This book belongs to

Age

Favourite player

Prediction of Bolton Wanderers' final position this season

Prediction of Sky Bet Championship winners this season

Prediction of FA Cup winners this season

Prediction of Capital One Cup winners this season

Written by twocan

Contributors: Danie
Theo Squires & Rob Mason

A TWOCAN PUBLICATION

ISBN 978-1-909872-54-7

PICTURE CREDITS
Back Page Images,
Action Images, Mirrorpix.

£8

CONTENTS

THE SQUAD 2015/16

01 BEN AMOS

Position: Goalkeeper **Nationality:** English
DOB: 10.04.90

A former England Under-21 international, Wanderers brought in Amos on loan from Manchester United in January 2015 and he returned this summer, signing a four-year contract with the club.

02 PRINCE-DESIRE GOUANO

Position: Defender **Nationality:** French
DOB: 24.12.93

Prince signed in August 2015 on loan from Italian club Atalanta. He won the Trotters' Player of the Month award after spending less than four weeks with the club! He has also represented France at U18, U19 and U20 levels.

03 DEAN MOXEY

Position: Defender **Nationality:** English
DOB: 14.01.86

Moxey signed for Wanderers in the summer of 2014, on a free transfer from Crystal Palace. He scored his first Bolton goal against Charlton Athletic in October 2014 before cementing his first team place in 2015/16.

JOSH VELA

06

Position: Midfielder Nationality: English
DOB: 14.12.93

Vela has emerged as a promising prospect for the Whites since signing professional terms with the club in March 2011. He has shown his versatility and established himself as a Wanderers regular last season.

DORIAN DERVITE

04

Position: Defender Nationality: French
DOB: 25.07.88

Initially on the subs' bench at the start of last season, his first campaign with the club, an injury to David Wheater allowed Dervite to establish himself as first choice in the Whites' back-line alongside Matt Mills.

LIAM FEENEY

07

Position: Midfielder Nationality: English
DOB: 28.04.86

The flying winger impressed during a loan stint with Bolton early in the 2013/14 campaign and the Whites moved quickly to tie up a permanent two year deal in the summer of 2014. He instantly established himself as a regular in midfield.

JAY SPEARING 08

Position: Midfielder Nationality: English
DOB: 25.11.88

Spearing had spent most of his career at his home club Liverpool before signing with Bolton on August 8, 2013. He made his debut the following day in the 1-1 home draw against Reading, in which he got Man of the Match.

ZACH CLOUGH 10

Position: Striker Nationality: English
DOB: 08.03.95

A graduate of Bolton's youth academy and a regular for Wanderers' Under-21s, highly-rated striker Zach Clough scored on his Wanderers debut against Wigan Athletic in January 2015, before cementing his place in Neil Lennon's first team.

MAX CLAYTON 12

Position: Striker Nationality: English
DOB: 09.01.95

An England youth international, Clayton joined Wanderers in September 2014. After a bright start to last season, a knee injury suffered against Ipswich Town ended his campaign prematurely in December 2014.

PAUL RACHUBKA 13

Position: Goalkeeper Nationality: American
DOB: 21.05.81

An experienced shot stopper with over 15 years' experience, Rachubka put pen to paper on a one-year contract at Macron Stadium. He is set to provide competition for Ben Amos and Ross Fitzsimons until the end of the season.

GARY MADINE 14

Position: Striker Nationality: English
DOB: 24.08.90

A product of Carlisle United's youth academy, Madine joined Bolton this summer on a two-year deal after being released by Sheffield Wednesday. He made over 100 appearances for the Owls alongside temporary loan spells.

DERIK OSEDE 15

Position: Defender Nationality: Spanish
DOB: 21.02.93

Derik penned a three-year deal with Bolton in July 2015. He has represented the Spanish national team at every level between U16 and U21 and has been a mainstay in the Real Madrid Castilla team for the previous two seasons.

LIAM TROTTER 17

Position: Midfielder Nationality: English
DOB: 24.08.88

Trotter joined Wanderers in July 2014 after a successful loan spell. He won the Whites' goal of the season for 2013/14 after a memorable long-range shot against Sheffield Wednesday at Hillsborough.

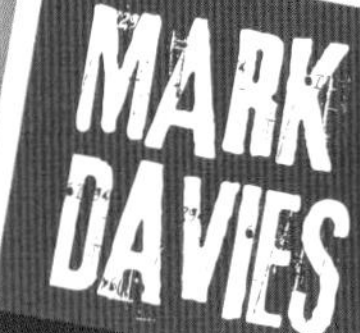

MARK DAVIES 16

Position: Midfielder Nationality: English
DOB: 18.02.88

A former England youth international and a highly-rated midfielder, Davies moved to Bolton in January 2009 from Wolverhampton Wanderers. He is the club's current longest-serving player and vice-captain.

NEIL DANNS 18

Position: Midfielder Nationality: Guyanese
DOB: 23.11.82

A seasoned professional having been involved in the game for over a decade, Danns has enjoyed stints with Blackburn Rovers, Colchester United, Birmingham City and Crystal Palace as well as representing the Guyana national team.

EMILE HESKEY

19

Position: Striker Nationality: English
DOB: 11.01.78

Heskey's career stretches over 20 years and his name is synonymous with the Premier League and England side. He established his place in the hearts of Bolton fans, scoring on his debut against Blackburn Rovers in December 2014.

DARREN PRATLEY

21

Position: Midfielder Nationality: English
DOB: 22.04.85

Pratley established himself as one of the first names on the Whites' teamsheet following the arrival of Neil Lennon as manager in October 2014. He was named the new Bolton Wanderers captain at the start of the 2015/16 season.

JOSE MANUEL CASADO

20

Position: Defender Nationality: Spanish
DOB: 09.08.86

Bolton signed Casado in September 2015. He has spent his whole career in Spain, after progressing though the youth ranks at Sevilla and Barcelona before going on to represent Sevilla, Recreativo, Xerez, Rayo Vallecano, Malaga and Almeria.

STEPHEN DOBBIE 23

Position: Striker Nationality: Scottish
DOB: 05.12.82

Dobbie joined the Trotters on a one-year contract this summer following a successful trial. He has previously won promotion to the Premier League three times in the last six campaigns with Blackpool, Swansea City and Crystal Palace!

WELLINGTON SILVA 22

Position: Midfielder Nationality: Brazilian
DOB: 06.01.93

A Brazilian U21 international, Silva joined Bolton on a season-long loan deal this summer from Arsenal having spent the last five seasons on loan in Spain to a number of clubs. He is capable of playing as both a winger or a second striker.

FRANCESCO PISANO 24

Position: Defender Nationality: Italian
DOB: 24.09.86

Pisano signed a two-year contract after completing a free transfer to the Trotters this summer. He has spent his entire career in Serie A with Cagliari, but left the Italian club at the end of his contract following their relegation to Serie B.

FILIP TWARDZIK 27

Position: Defender Nationality: Czech
DOB: 10.02.93

Twardzik was reunited with his former Celtic manager Neil Lennon when he signed for Bolton in February 2015. He scored on his debut, coming off the bench against Derby County and heading home Barry Bannan's free-kick.

LAWRIE WILSON 25

Position: Defender Nationality: English
DOB: 11.09.87

Wilson signed a two-year contract this summer from Charlton Athletic, following a successful trial period. A versatile defender, he is equally capable of playing on either flank in both defence and midfield.

KAIYNE WOOLERY 30

Position: Striker Nationality: English
DOB: 11.01.95

A summer-signing from Conference side Tamworth in August 2014, Woolery impressed for Wanderers' Under-21s in his first season with the club and was rewarded with a first team debut against AFC Bournemouth in April 2015.

DAVID WHEATER 31

Position: Defender Nationality: English
DOB: 14.02.87

A former England Under-21s international, Wheater joined the Whites in January 2011. One of the club's most experienced players, he captained the Whites on occasions last season.

HAYDEN WHITE 33

Position: Defender Nationality: English
DOB: 15.04.95

A regular for Wanderers' Under-21s side since his arrival in June 2013, White spent the majority of last season out on loan and will be looking to cement a place in the first team following his return to Macron Stadium.

TOM EAVES 32

Position: Striker Nationality: English
DOB: 14.01.92

A powerhouse centre-forward, Eaves joined Bolton Wanderers in the summer of 2010 from Oldham Athletic for an undisclosed fee. He has taken in a number of loan spells recently, gaining valuable experience.

ALEX FINNEY 36

Position: Defender Nationality: English
DOB: 06.06.96

A talented centre-back, Finney joined Bolton Wanderers from Leyton Orient in August 2014. He made his first team debut as a substitute against Huddersfield Town in September 2015.

ROSS FITZSIMONS 34

Position: Goalkeeper Nationality: English
DOB: 28.05.94

Fitzsimons has been providing cover and competition for the first choice 'keepers and has been on the bench for a number of first team fixtures. He has also been establishing himself as the development squad's number one shot stopper.

CONOR WILKINSON 35

Position: Striker Nationality: English
DOB: 23.01.95

Wilkinson joined Bolton Wanderers in the summer of 2013. He has taken in loan spells at Chester, Torquay United, Oldham Athletic and most recently, Barnsley. He has also been capped for Republic of Ireland at youth level.

QUADE TAYLOR 37

Position: Defender **Nationality:** English
DOB: 11.12.93

A regular for Bolton Wanderers' Under-21s last season, Taylor's impressive displays for the young Whites saw him handed his senior debut by manager Neil Lennon against Birmingham City on the final day of the 2014/15 campaign.

OSCAR THRELKELD 41

Position: Defender **Nationality:** English
DOB: 15.12.94

A product of the club's academy, Threlkeld made his first team bow against Sheffield Wednesday in April 2014. He has figured prominently for the Under-21 side in recent years and also captained them a number of times last season.

TOM WALKER 42

Position: Midfielder **Nationality:** English
DOB: 12.12.95

A versatile midfielder who progressed through the Whites' academy. Walker was the youngest member of the first team squad last season and established himself as a regular during the latter stages of the campaign.

ROB HOLDING 45

Position: Defender **Nationality:** English
DOB: 20.09.95

Holding has progressed through the youth ranks at Bolton. He spent time on loan at League Two Bury last season gaining valuable experience and made his Whites debut in August 2015 in a League Cup defeat to Burton Albion.

MEDO KAMARA 44

Position: Midfielder **Nationality:** Sierra Leonean
DOB: 16.11.87

A defensive midfielder born and raised in Sierra Leone, Kamara joined Bolton in January 2013 from Partizan Belgrade on a three-and-a-half year deal. He also represents the Sierra Leone national team.

NIALL MAHER 48

Position: Defender **Nationality:** English
DOB: 31.07.95

Maher has been with Wanderers since the age of ten but has yet to make his first team debut. He joined Blackpool on a one-month loan in January 2015 and he made his Football League debut against Watford at Vicarage Road.

Dick Pym (centre)

Eddie Hopkinson

Jussi Jaaskelainen

Eddie Hopkinson

Having made a club record 578 appearances, goalkeeper Eddie Hopkinson is one of Bolton Wanderers' biggest legends.

He signed for the Whites in August 1952 when just 16 years of age, but would have to wait until 1956 before being handed his maiden Bolton appearance - coming in a 4-1 victory over local-rivals Blackpool.

His form for the Trotters earned him a senior England debut against Wales in October 1957, while he was also a member of the Three Lions squad that competed in the 1958 World Cup.

An FA Cup winner with Wanderers in 1958 after keeping a clean sheet against Manchester United in the final, he remained the Whites' first-choice goalkeeper throughout the 1960s before injury ended his career.

A hospitality host at the Reebok Stadium during his later years having previously served as Bolton's assistant trainer and goalkeeping coach in the 1970s, Hopkinson has a box at BL6 named in his honour, while he was an inaugural member of the Whites' Hall of Fame.

Dick Pym

Nicknamed 'Pincher' Pym, three-time FA Cup winner Dick Pym made over 300 appearances for Wanderers in ten seasons with the club during the 1920s.

Moving to the Whites from Exeter City in July 1921 for a club-record £5000, he was an ever-present for Bolton during the 1922/23 season as they lifted the FA Cup for the first time in the club's history.

Facing West Ham United in the first ever final at Wembley, Pym kept a clean sheet as the Trotters clinched a famous 2-0 victory.

Handed his England debut against Wales in February 1925, he would win three caps for the Three Lions.

The following year he lifted the FA Cup for a second time, before making it a hat-trick of winners' medals in 1929, keeping clean sheets in both of Wanderers' victories over Manchester City and Portsmouth.

Making his last Whites appearance in 1930, Pym worked in the fishing industry following his retirement, while he was the last surviving member of Bolton's historic 1923 side.

Jussi Jaaskelainen

One of many modern day legends to have graced the Reebok Stadium turf, Jussi Jaaskelainen established himself as one of the Premier League's finest goalkeepers during his 15-year stint with Wanderers.

Brought to England by Colin Todd in November 1997, the big Finn started the 1998/99 season as the Whites' first-choice goalkeeper, before firmly cementing his place as a virtual ever-present following Bolton's promotion to the Premiership in 2000/01.

With his heroics in goal initially helping the Trotters avoid relegation, Jaaskelainen continued to star as Wanderers reached the Carling Cup Final in 2004 before competing in the UEFA Cup in 2005/06 and 2007/08.

Making his 500th Whites appearance in their FA Cup quarter-final victory over Birmingham City in March 2011, injuries saw Jaasekelainen lose his place in goal the following year as Bolton suffered relegation.

Moving to West Ham United on a free transfer, he spent three years in the capital before signing for League One Wigan Athletic at the start of the 2015/16 season.

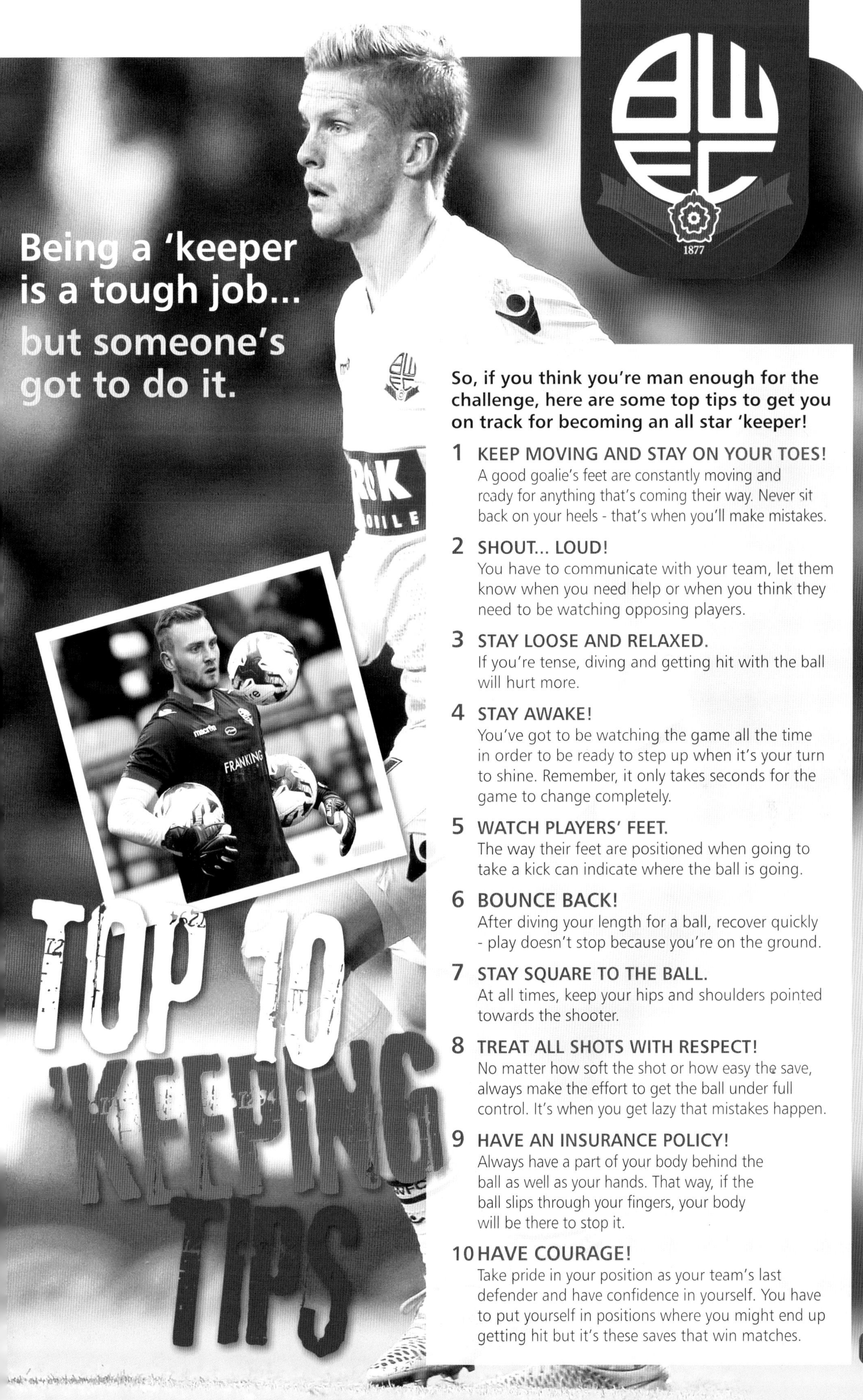

Being a 'keeper is a tough job... but someone's got to do it.

TOP 10 'KEEPING TIPS

So, if you think you're man enough for the challenge, here are some top tips to get you on track for becoming an all star 'keeper!

1. **KEEP MOVING AND STAY ON YOUR TOES!**
   A good goalie's feet are constantly moving and ready for anything that's coming their way. Never sit back on your heels - that's when you'll make mistakes.
2. **SHOUT... LOUD!**
   You have to communicate with your team, let them know when you need help or when you think they need to be watching opposing players.
3. **STAY LOOSE AND RELAXED.**
   If you're tense, diving and getting hit with the ball will hurt more.
4. **STAY AWAKE!**
   You've got to be watching the game all the time in order to be ready to step up when it's your turn to shine. Remember, it only takes seconds for the game to change completely.
5. **WATCH PLAYERS' FEET.**
   The way their feet are positioned when going to take a kick can indicate where the ball is going.
6. **BOUNCE BACK!**
   After diving your length for a ball, recover quickly - play doesn't stop because you're on the ground.
7. **STAY SQUARE TO THE BALL.**
   At all times, keep your hips and shoulders pointed towards the shooter.
8. **TREAT ALL SHOTS WITH RESPECT!**
   No matter how soft the shot or how easy the save, always make the effort to get the ball under full control. It's when you get lazy that mistakes happen.
9. **HAVE AN INSURANCE POLICY!**
   Always have a part of your body behind the ball as well as your hands. That way, if the ball slips through your fingers, your body will be there to stop it.
10. **HAVE COURAGE!**
    Take pride in your position as your team's last defender and have confidence in yourself. You have to put yourself in positions where you might end up getting hit but it's these saves that win matches.

GOAL OF THE YEAR

Bolton Wanderers' top goal of the 2014/15 season came from the right boot of Mark Davies following a moment of individual brilliance from the Whites' longest-serving player.

Facing off against Brentford in Neil Lennon's first game at Macron Stadium in October 2014, Bolton were keen to impress in front of the home fans under their new manager, and took the lead just after the hour-mark courtesy of Neil Danns' superb 30-yard strike.

With the game remaining in the balance as it headed into its final quarter, Lennon looked to his bench, seeking a man to bring on to swing the tide in Wanderers' favour. Enter Mark Davies.

Having seen the start of his campaign stunted by injuries, the playmaker did not disappoint after entering the field - wasting no time in making an immediate impact. Within two minutes of coming on, Davies controlled a weak Brentford clearance on his chest on the edge of the penalty area before embarking on a run at goal.

Instantly shrugging off two Bees' challenges, the former England youth international turned brilliantly to beat his man after bursting into the box, before weaving past a further two Brentford players and calmly slotting the ball beneath goalkeeper David Button's grasp into the bottom right-hand corner to double the Whites' lead.

And although Jon Toral pulled one back for the visitors in the final ten minutes, fellow substitute Craig Davies sealed the points in injury-time, slotting home from 40-yards after Button was caught out of position after joining the attack for a late Brentford corner.

While all three Bolton goals that day would rank highly against any other come the end of the campaign, it was Mark Davies' solo-effort that stood out as he created an opportunity out of nothing before finishing in memorable fashion.

1877
macron
ROK
MOBILE
BWFC
mitre
DARREN
PRATLEY
21

FULL NAME?
Dorian Dervite

NICKNAME?
Dozza

CHILDHOOD TEAM?
RC Lens

CHILDHOOD HERO?
Batman

YOUR BEST ATTRIBUTE AS A PLAYER?
Defending

THE HIGHLIGHT OF YOUR CAREER SO FAR?
Playing at Anfield and Stamford Bridge

THE FAVOURITE GOAL YOU HAVE SCORED?
Against Bournemouth with Charlton, it helped us stay in the Championship

DESCRIBE YOURSELF IN THREE WORDS?
Friendly, quiet, laid-back

FAVOURITE AWAY GROUND?
Anfield

BEST FRIEND IN FOOTBALL?
Yann Kermorgant

DRAW A QUICK SELF PORTRAIT...

FULL NAME?
David James Wheater

NICKNAME?
Wheatz

CHILDHOOD TEAM?
Middlesbrough

CHILDHOOD HERO?
Stone Cold Steve Austin

YOUR BEST ATTRIBUTE AS A PLAYER?
Fearlessness

THE HIGHLIGHT OF YOUR CAREER SO FAR?
My England call-up

THE FAVOURITE GOAL YOU HAVE SCORED?
Two goals vs Blackburn

DESCRIBE YOURSELF IN THREE WORDS?
What a player

FAVOURITE AWAY GROUND?
Old Trafford

BEST FRIEND IN FOOTBALL?
Robert Lainton

DRAW A QUICK SELF PORTRAIT...

DRAW A QUICK SELF PORTRAIT...

FULL NAME?
Dean Moxey

NICKNAME?
Mox

CHILDHOOD TEAM?
Man United

CHILDHOOD HERO?
Ryan Giggs

YOUR BEST ATTRIBUTE AS A PLAYER?
Running around

THE HIGHLIGHT OF YOUR CAREER SO FAR?
Promotion to the Premier League

THE FAVOURITE GOAL YOU HAVE SCORED?
Exeter City v Doncaster, FA Cup Round 2

DESCRIBE YOURSELF IN THREE WORDS?
Chilled out entertainer

FAVOURITE AWAY GROUND?
Emirates

BEST FRIEND IN FOOTBALL?
Darren Ambrose

FULL NAME?
Emile William Ivanhoe Heskey

NICKNAME?
Ems / Emi

CHILDHOOD TEAM?
Liverpool

CHILDHOOD HERO?
John Barnes, Ian Wright, Romario

YOUR BEST ATTRIBUTE AS A PLAYER?
Strength

THE HIGHLIGHT OF YOUR CAREER SO FAR?
5-1 for England away at Germany in a World Cup qualifier

THE FAVOURITE GOAL YOU HAVE SCORED?
5-1 for England away at Germany in a World Cup qualifier

DESCRIBE YOURSELF IN THREE WORDS?
Quiet, honest, caring

FAVOURITE AWAY GROUND?
Anfield

BEST FRIEND IN FOOTBALL?
Too many!

TEAM TALK

16

MARK DAVIES

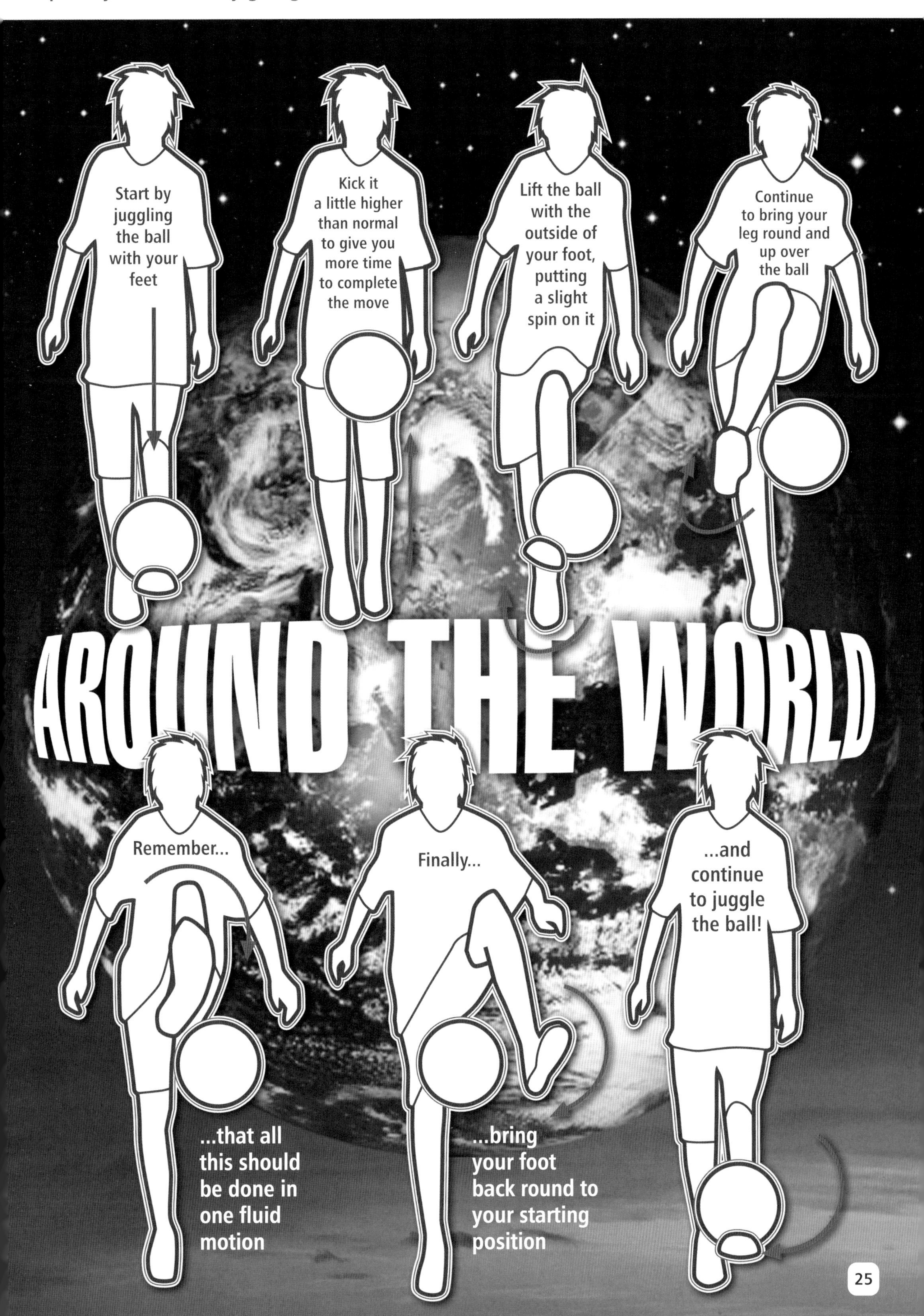

Start by juggling the ball with your feet
Kick it a little higher than normal to give you more time to complete the move
Lift the ball with the outside of your foot, putting a slight spin on it
Continue to bring your leg round and up over the ball
AROUND THE WORLD
Remember...
...that all this should be done in one fluid motion
Finally...
...bring your foot back round to your starting position
...and continue to juggle the ball!

1877
FibrLec
ROK
MOBILE
macron

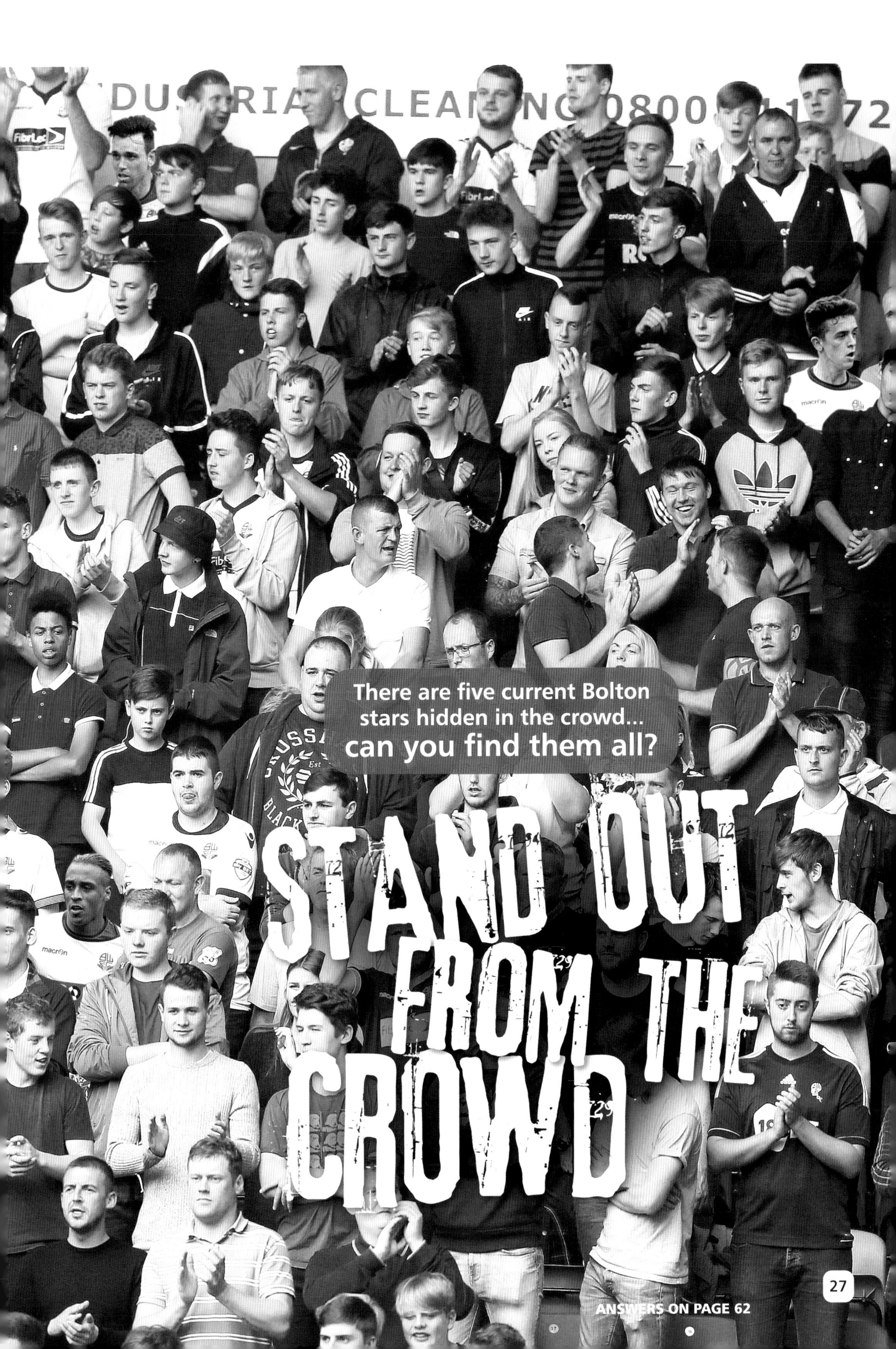
There are five current Bolton stars hidden in the crowd...
can you find them all?
STAND OUT FROM THE CROWD

ANSWERS ON PAGE 62

Being a defender is a hard task... are you man enough?

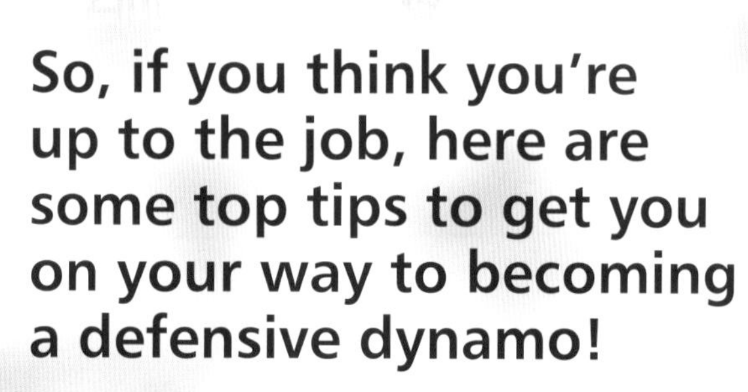

So, if you think you're up to the job, here are some top tips to get you on your way to becoming a defensive dynamo!

1. **APPLY PRESSURE!**
   Badger the attacking side constantly to force them to make mistakes, make life as difficult as you can for them. It's hard to score goals when you're under pressure.
2. **BE ON THE BALL!**
   Stay on your toes and be ready to sprint for a stray ball at any time.
3. **MARK YOUR MAN!**
   Always know where your attacker is, never let him get behind you or you'll lose sight of the ball.
4. **KEEP YOUR EYES ON THE PRIZE.**
   Don't let the ball out of your sight, that way, it can't sneak up on you! Also, watch your attacker's feet to anticipate what they will do next.
5. **KEEP IN TOUCH WITH YOUR GOALIE.**
   He often has a better view of what is going on on the pitch and will be able to direct you.
6. **DON'T DIVE IN RECKLESSLY!**
   If you haven't got a good view of the ball, don't dive or slide in, you'll only get yourself into bother.
7. **NEVER GIVE UP!**
   Keep moving, if an attacker has got past you, go after him, fast!
8. **BE TOUGH!**
   Tackle hard and fast, but always go for the ball, not the man.
9. **WATCH THE GAME!**
   Always be aware and watch for passes you can intercept.
10. **WORK AS A TEAM!**
    If a fellow defender is working on an attacker, be there to support him. You need to be around to provide back-up if the attacker gets past him.

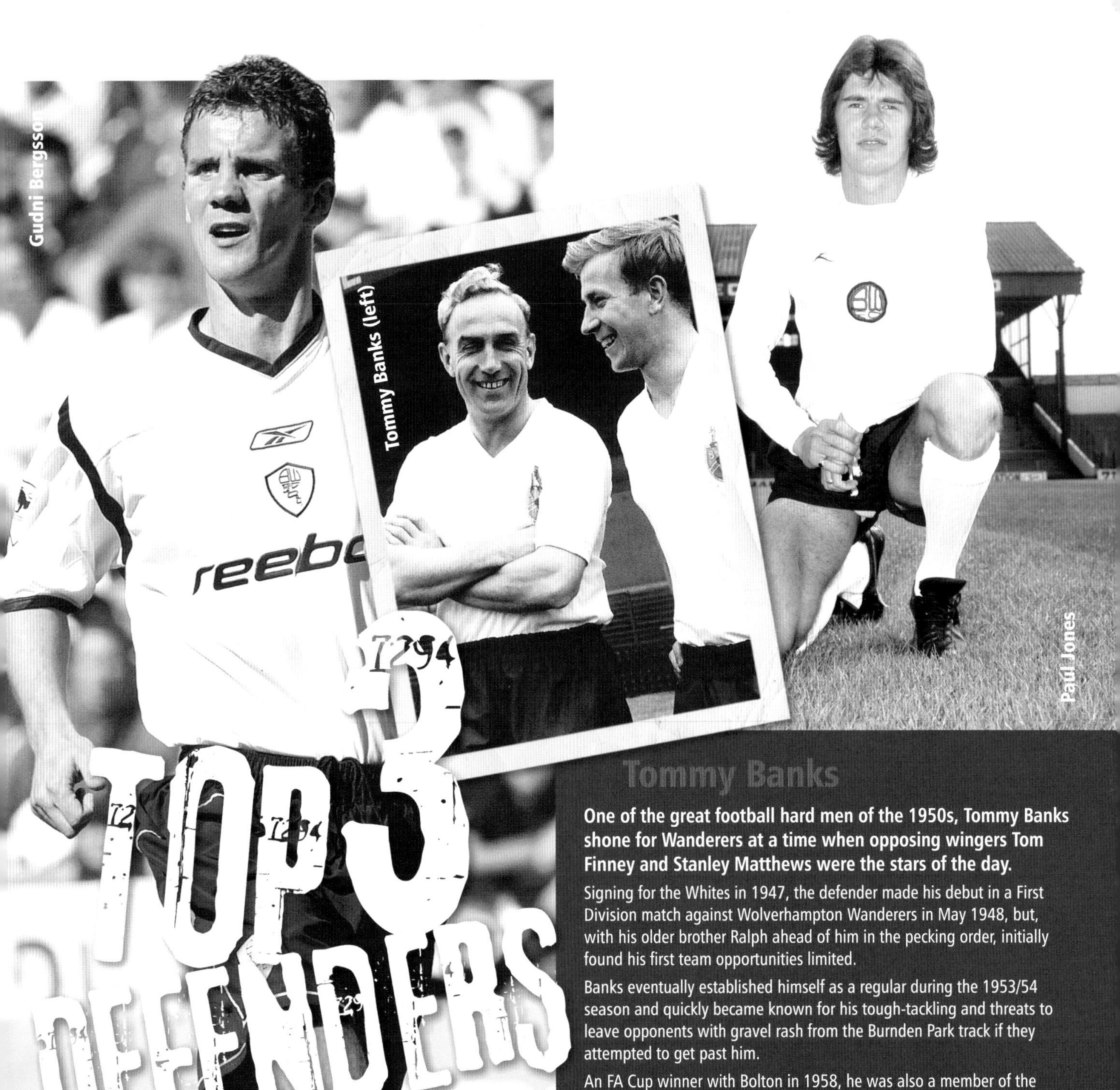

Tommy Banks

One of the great football hard men of the 1950s, Tommy Banks shone for Wanderers at a time when opposing wingers Tom Finney and Stanley Matthews were the stars of the day.

Signing for the Whites in 1947, the defender made his debut in a First Division match against Wolverhampton Wanderers in May 1948, but, with his older brother Ralph ahead of him in the pecking order, initially found his first team opportunities limited.

Banks eventually established himself as a regular during the 1953/54 season and quickly became known for his tough-tackling and threats to leave opponents with gravel rash from the Burnden Park track if they attempted to get past him.

An FA Cup winner with Bolton in 1958, he was also a member of the England squad that competed in the 1958 World Cup, starting all four of the Three Lions' matches, before later leaving Trotters at the end of the 1960/61 season having made over 250 appearances for the club.

Gudni Bergsson

Firmly regarded as an adopted Boltonian, Gudni Bergsson won promotion to the Premier League three times under three different managers during his time with Wanderers.

Signing from Tottenham Hotspur in March 1995, the Iceland international made his Whites debut in the Coca-Cola Cup Final against Liverpool - helping create Alan Thompson's consolation strike.

Returning to Wembley for the Division One Play-Off Final, he started as Bolton secured a famous 4-3 victory over Reading, before winning promotion to the Premiership again in 1996/97, this time as champions, in the Trotters' final ever season at Burnden Park.

Twice persuaded to postpone retirement plans by Sam Allardyce, Bergsson scored ten goals in 2000/01 as Wanderers won promotion to the Premiership for a third time after beating Preston North End in the Play-Off Final.

He then made 61 league appearances over the next two seasons as the Whites twice avoided the drop, before hanging up his boots in 2003 to become a certified lawyer in his native Iceland.

Paul Jones

Having twice won promotion with Wanderers during the seventies, stylish centre-back Paul Jones ensured he was one of the first names on the Whites teamsheet throughout the decade, having come through the club's junior ranks.

Signing for the club as an apprentice in 1969, he was handed his league debut when only 17-years old against Sheffield United in January 1971.

Following a stint in midfield during his breakthrough season in 1971/72, he soon dropped back into defence and was an ever-present as Bolton won promotion to the Second Division as champions in 1973.

Missing just one league game between 1974 and 1977, Jones helped the Trotters win promotion to the top-flight in 1977/78, while also showing his versatility with stints at right-back.

A prolific goalscorer from the back, his form for Wanderers would also earn him an England call-up under Don Revie.

Jones made his 500th Whites appearance against Rotherham United in February 1983, appearing just a further six times before ending his 14-year association with the club.

PLAYER OF THE YEAR

American international Tim Ream was named Bolton Wanderers' Player of the Season for the second year running in 2014/15, with his consistent displays not going unnoticed by the Whites supporters.

Voted for by the fans, the defender was a virtual ever-present during the campaign, appearing in 49 of Wanderers' 52 matches over the course of the year.

Known for his reliability and consistency, Ream also often showed his versatility as he filled in as a defensive midfielder or even at right-back on occasions, as well as being fielded in his favoured positions at left-back and centre-back.

A winter signing from MLS side New York Red Bulls in January 2012, Ream cancelled his honeymoon so that the deal could go through, having impressed during a brief trial with the Whites the month before.

Despite a slow start to his Trotters career, he established himself as a mainstay in the Bolton defence during the 2013/14 season.

Ream's performances would see him named as the Trotters' Player of the Year for the first time, while he was also nominated for the Sky Bet Championship Player of the Year at the North West Football Awards.

But despite his impressive form on the pitch, he was surprisingly not included in Jurgen Klinsmann's USA squad for the 2014 World Cup in Brazil.

Bouncing back from his international disappointment, Ream maintained his high standards of the previous year as he again lifted the Wanderers' Player of the Year accolade, while a second NWFAwards Sky Bet Championship Player of the Year nomination also followed.

With his performances earning him an international recall as well as a place in the USA squad for the CONCACAF 2015 Gold Cup, Ream called time on his Whites career in August 2015 as he joined Fulham having made 126 appearances during his three-and -a-half years at Macron Stadium.

BEN AMOS

GUESS THE CLUB

Can you work out which Championship club each set of clues is pointing to?

1

ANSWER

2

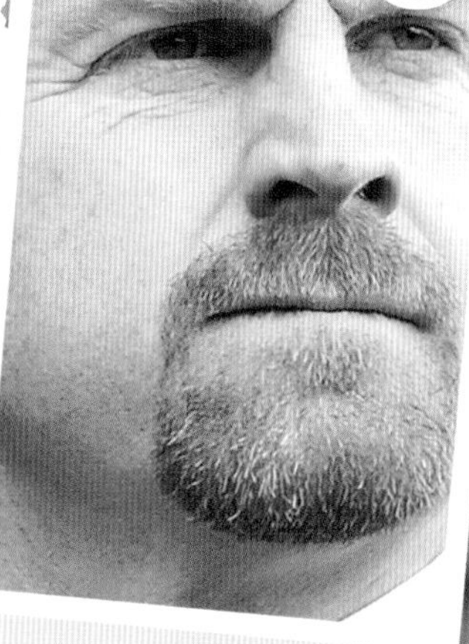

ANSWER

3

ANSWER

4

ANSWER

ANSWERS ON PAGE 62

10

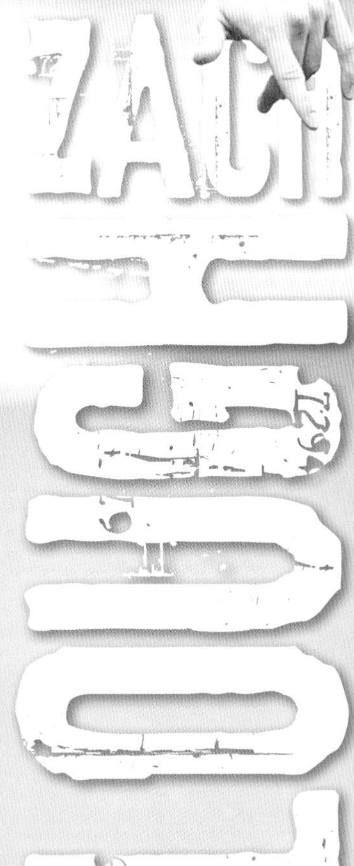

Here are the nicknames of every Championship Club. Can you work out who the team is and then find them in the grid?

P	H	U	D	D	E	R	S	F	I	E	L	D	T	O	W	N	O	C	N	C	Q
A	R	I	S	E	P	M	M	E	G	T	H	U	H	A	O	A	B	I	B	H	U
U	A	E	L	Y	T	I	C	L	O	T	S	I	R	B	L	W	H	H	E	A	E
L	I	P	S	W	I	C	H	T	O	W	N	S	K	M	V	S	G	U	C	R	E
A	T	M	G	T	K	B	A	F	R	B	F	N	B	H	E	T	U	L	Z	L	N
Q	S	Y	P	E	O	L	U	K	G	N	I	D	A	E	R	R	O	L	P	T	S
W	E	T	I	E	B	N	H	R	U	S	T	P	E	O	H	T	R	C	S	O	P
B	R	I	G	H	T	O	N	A	N	D	H	O	V	E	A	L	B	I	O	N	A
I	O	C	I	D	I	G	R	O	A	L	C	S	I	H	M	U	S	T	S	A	R
R	F	F	Y	V	J	A	D	Q	R	C	E	J	A	V	P	S	E	Y	Q	T	K
M	M	F	D	G	W	K	F	O	C	T	I	Y	T	S	T	K	L	T	U	H	R
I	A	I	O	F	M	S	E	G	U	O	H	B	K	A	O	I	D	I	W	L	A
N	H	D	D	E	T	I	N	U	S	D	E	E	L	S	N	R	D	G	H	E	N
G	G	R	A	N	K	E	M	D	V	A	U	E	N	D	W	O	I	E	W	T	G
H	N	A	N	F	C	A	N	Z	L	F	B	I	S	D	A	Y	M	R	S	I	E
A	I	C	T	J	H	D	R	O	F	T	N	E	R	B	N	D	Q	S	R	C	R
M	T	X	O	L	C	B	O	L	T	O	N	W	A	N	D	E	R	E	R	S	S
C	T	Y	U	Y	A	D	S	E	N	D	E	W	D	L	E	I	F	F	E	H	S
I	O	F	M	W	U	J	Y	T	N	U	O	C	Y	B	R	E	D	B	E	X	Y
T	N	P	B	L	A	C	K	B	U	R	N	R	O	V	E	R	S	P	G	I	A
Y	D	E	T	I	N	U	M	A	H	R	E	H	T	O	R	V	I	W	K	O	N
								Y	M	P	L	O	N	E	S	Y	C	S	W	B	H

NAME THAT TEAM...

1. Robins ____________
2. Rovers ____________
3. Royals ____________
4. Boro ____________
5. Cottagers ____________
6. Clarets ____________
7. Bluebirds ____________
8. Blues ____________
9. Seagulls ____________
10. Terriers ____________
11. Bees ____________
12. Tigers ____________
13. Whites ____________
14. Hoops ____________
15. The Dons ____________
16. Wolves ____________
17. Millers ____________
18. Owls ____________
19. Forest ____________
20. Trotters ____________
21. Lilywhites ____________
22. Tractor Boys ____________
23. Addicks ____________
24. Rams ____________

ANSWERS ON PAGE 62

Footballers are getting fitter and fitter. Just as athletics records are broken, as runners get faster and faster, in football each generation of players are faster, fitter and stronger than before.

Clubs have more and more support staff, to provide everything a player will need to help him become the supreme athlete. These days, teams have fitness & conditioning coaches and nutritionists, who make sure every player is in the best physical shape he can be.

In pre-season, clubs carry out all kinds of tests on their players to monitor their progress and ensure each individual reaches and maintains peak fitness. A lot of work is done in the gym with weights, designed to make sure players have the strength not to be easily knocked off the ball and that they also possess the stamina to get through 90 minutes and not fade in the game's latter stages.

Of course, while fitness is essential, ultimately it is their ability that matters. Footballers like to train with the ball and work hard on their skills. A lot of drills are undertaken to develop and maintain each player's ability on the ball. Coaching staff also work on team play, formations and developing understandings on the pitch.

A large proportion of goals come from set-pieces, so teams work on not just taking them, but defending free-kicks, corners and throw ins. Every team has a specialist dead-ball expert who they rely on for these important moments in games. Some teams prefer to do man-for-man marking and some use the zonal approach. In man-for-man marking, every player has a responsibility to mark a particular opponent, while zonal marking means, every player has an area of the pitch that they have to defend.

Whichever system is used, it is important that players work hard in training, so that they are a fully fit and well organised unit, and can perform together, successfully as a team.

TRAIN
TO WIN
BWFC
1877
NL
macron
FRANKI
SENSE
FRANKING
Catapult
14
7
8

MEET YOUR RIVALS

Birmingham City

GROUND: St Andrew's CAPACITY: 30,016

MANAGER: Gary Rowett NICKNAME: Blues

DID YOU KNOW: Founded as Small Heath, they played in the Football Alliance before becoming founder members and first ever champions of the Football League Second Division.

Blackburn Rovers

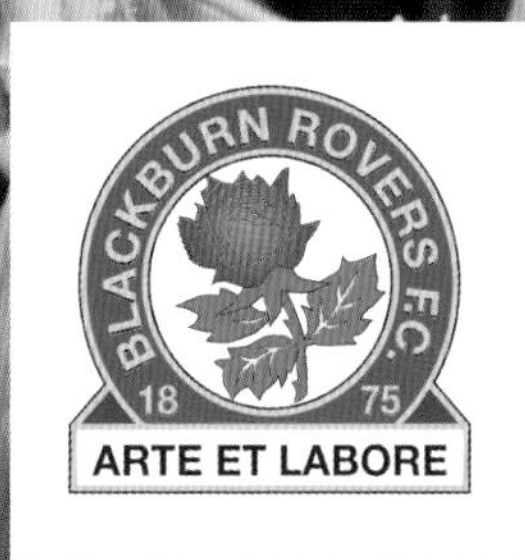

GROUND: Ewood Park CAPACITY: 31,367

MANAGER: Gary Bowyer NICKNAME: Rovers

DID YOU KNOW:
Blackburn Rovers' Latin motto is 'Arte et labore', the Club's translation of which is 'By Skill and Hard Work'.

Brentford

GROUND: Griffin Park CAPACITY: 12,300

MANAGER: Marinus Dijkhuizen NICKNAME: The Bees

DID YOU KNOW:
Brentford's most successful spell came during the 1930s, when they achieved consecutive top six finishes in the First Division.

Brighton & Hove Albion

GROUND: The Amex Stadium CAPACITY: 30,750

MANAGER: Chris Hughton NICKNAME: The Seagulls

DID YOU KNOW: Brighton have a number of celebrity fans, including commentator Des Lynam, DJ Fat Boy Slim and comic genius Norman Wisdom.

Bristol City

GROUND: Ashton Gate

CAPACITY: Upgrading to 27,000 by 2016

MANAGER: Steve Cotterill NICKNAME: The Robins

DID YOU KNOW: Bristol City won the Welsh Cup - despite being an English club - in 1934.

Burnley

GROUND: Turf Moor **CAPACITY:** 21,401

MANAGER: Sean Dyche **NICKNAME:** The Clarets

DID YOU KNOW:
Burnley's club colours of claret and blue were adopted in 1910 in tribute to the best club in English football at the time, Aston Villa.

Cardiff City

GROUND: Cardiff City Stadium **CAPACITY:** 33,280

MANAGER: Russell Slade **NICKNAME:** The Bluebirds

DID YOU KNOW:
Cardiff City is the only club from outside England to have won the FA Cup, which they won in 1927.

Charlton Athletic

GROUND: The Valley **CAPACITY:** 27,111

MANAGER: Guy Luzon **NICKNAME:** The Addicks

DID YOU KNOW:
Charlton were rare among football clubs, they reserved a seat on their directors' board for a supporter! (until 2008, when legal issues stopped them)

Derby County

GROUND: The iPro Stadium **CAPACITY:** 33,500

MANAGER: Paul Clement **NICKNAME:** The Rams

DID YOU KNOW:
Derby County's rival clubs are Nottingham Forest, Leicester City and Leeds United. Two of which they face this season!

Fulham

GROUND: Craven Cottage **CAPACITY:** 25,700

MANAGER: Kit Symons **NICKNAME:** The Cottagers

DID YOU KNOW: Fulham has produced many English greats including Johnny Haynes, George Cohen, Bobby Robson, Rodney Marsh & Alan Mullery.

Huddersfield Town

GROUND: John Smith's Stadium **CAPACITY:** 24,500

MANAGER: Chris Powell **NICKNAME:** The Terriers

DID YOU KNOW: In 1926, Huddersfield became the first English team to win three successive league titles - no team has beaten this record!

The writing's on the wall...

Decorate this wall and show your love for Bolton Wanderers

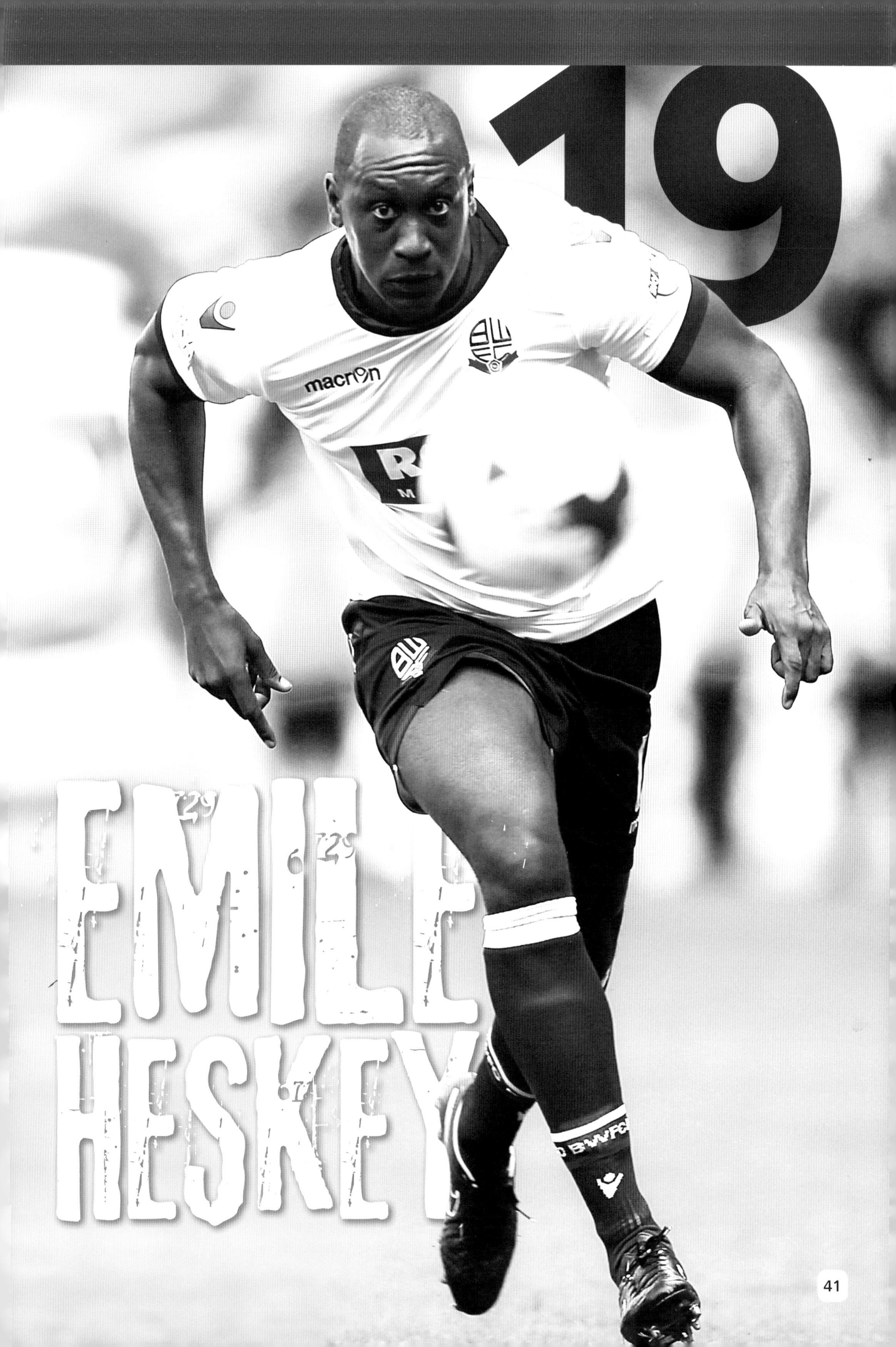
19
EMILE
HESKEY
macron

Can you identify these Bolton stars?

1

2

5

3

4

ANSWERS ON PAGE 62

GARY
MADINE
14

WHAT BALL?

A

B

There are too many balls in these action shots!
Can you figure out which balls are real?

ANSWERS ON PAGE 62

1877

Remember to swap roles with your friend so you both get a chance to work on your fitness!
START

You will need cones or markers, a ball and a friend!

Shuttle runs are a great fitness training exercise to help build speed, stamina, acceleration and endurance. Adding a football helps players control the ball at top speeds and when the body is tired.

EASY

Set up a line of 6-8 cones 5 metres apart. To begin with, run from the first cone to the second cone and back again. Next, run to the second cone and back again. Continue to do this until you have completed a run to the final cone.

HARD

Now, add a football into the mix!

Dribble from the start to the first cone, turn with the ball, pass back to your friend and then sprint back to the start. Your friend should stop the ball at the start where you will gain possession and dribble to the second cone. Repeat this process for each of the cones.

HARDER

There are many ways you can increase the difficulty level of this drill.

Have your friend throw the ball to you as you're running back to the start.

You will have to work to bring the ball under control, bring it back to the start and dribble on to the next cone - work on chest traps, thigh traps or traps with the feet.

As you improve, try and work faster. Can you invent some of your own ways to make this drill harder?

DRILLS: FITNESS

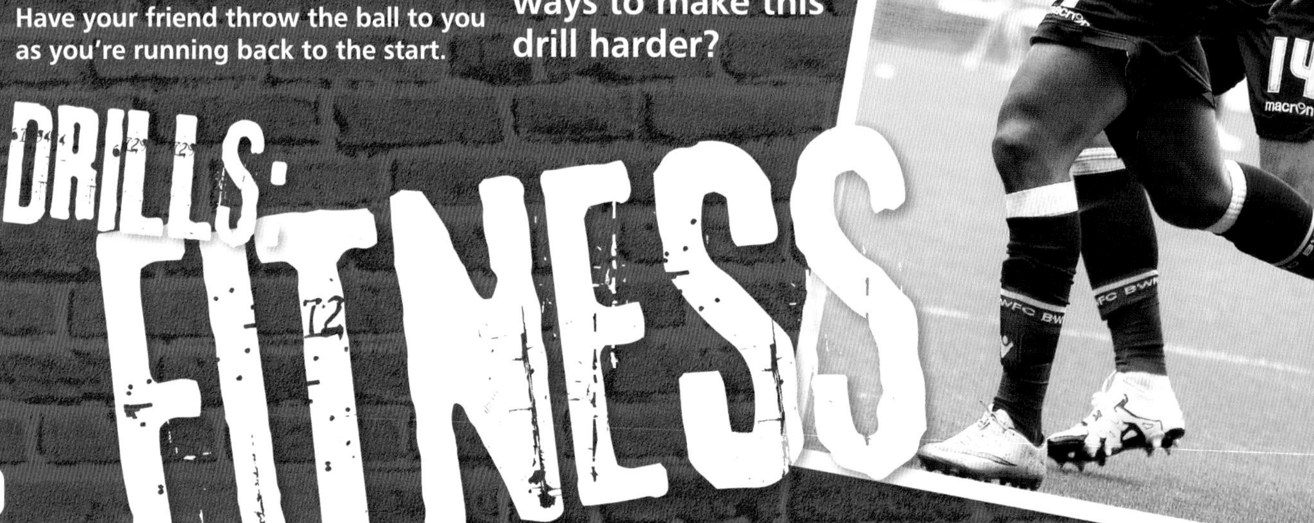
ROK MOBILE
macron
14

TOP 3 MIDFIELDERS

Jay-Jay Okocha

So good they named him twice, Jay-Jay Okocha is widely regarded as one of the most talented players to have ever pulled on a Bolton Wanderers shirt.

The talismanic playmaker signed for the Whites on a free transfer from Paris Saint-Germain in the summer of 2002, shortly after captaining Nigeria in the World Cup.

A firm fan-favourite, the Nigerian scored seven goals during an impressive first year in England, including crucial strikes against West Ham United and Middlesbrough as Bolton avoided relegation on the last day of the season.

Handed the captain's armband the following year, Okocha led the Trotters to the Carling Cup Final after scoring two goals in the semi-final against Aston Villa, before helping Wanderers qualify for the UEFA Cup for the first time in the club's history in 2004/05.

Leaving the Whites at the end of the 2005/06 season, Okocha left Bolton fans feeling privileged at having been able to watch one of the planet's greatest players showcase his talents on the Reebok Stadium turf.

Youri Djorkaeff

A World Cup and European Championships winner with France before rocking up at the Reebok Stadium, Youri Djorkaeff was one of the first great superstars to cross the channel to play for Wanderers.

Paving the way for future signings that Whites fans previously could only dream of, the Frenchman signed for Bolton from Kaiserslautern in February 2002.

Gifted with superb technique and silky skills, the attacking-midfielder's four goals in 12 appearances not only helped the Trotters avoid relegation, but also earned him an international recall for the 2002 World Cup, only for France to suffer a shock group-stage exit.

Extending his contract with Wanderers, he missed just two league games the following year, scoring seven goals, as the Whites again narrowly avoided relegation.

Djorakeff then netted a further ten in his final year with the club as Bolton finished in the top-half and reached the Carling Cup Final - recording back-to-back braces during his last month at Reebok Stadium to see out his Trotters career in style.

Roy Greaves

With 575 Wanderers appearances to his name, local boy Roy Greaves has turned out for the Whites more times than any other outfield player in the club's history.

Starting his career as a striker, he netted a brace on his Bolton home debut in a 3-2 victory over Southampton in October 1965 when just 18, having served his apprenticeship with the Trotters.

Establishing himself as a regular in 1967, Greaves scored double-figures in both 1967/68 and 1968/69 to finish as the club's leading goalscorer, before dropping into a deeper midfield role after Wanderers' relegation to the Third Division.

An ever-present in the side that won promotion to the Second Division as champions in 1973, he captained the Whites as they won a second promotion to reach the First Division, again as champions, in 1978.

Missing just one match in his first season in the top-flight, Greaves left the club the following year, bringing an end to his 15 years at Burnden Park.

Hull City

GROUND: KC Stadium **CAPACITY:** 25,450

MANAGER: Steve Bruce **NICKNAMES:** The Tigers

DID YOU KNOW:
Hull changed their club badge in June 2014, becoming one of few English league teams without the club name on their crest.

Ipswich Town

GROUND: Portman Road **CAPACITY:** 30,311

MANAGER: Mick McCarthy

NICKNAME: The Blues, The Tractor Boys

DID YOU KNOW: Ipswich last appeared in the Premier League in 2001/02, making them the Championship's longest-serving Club.

Leeds United

GROUND: Elland Road **CAPACITY:** 37,890

MANAGER: Uwe Rösler

NICKNAMES: The Whites, The Peacocks

DID YOU KNOW:
Leeds United fans have a salute which is known as the 'Leeds Salute'.

Middlesbrough

GROUND: Riverside Stadium **CAPACITY:** 34,742

MANAGER: Aitor Karanka

NICKNAMES: Boro, The Smoggies

DID YOU KNOW:
Middlesbrough won the League Cup in 2004, the club's first and only major trophy.

MK Dons

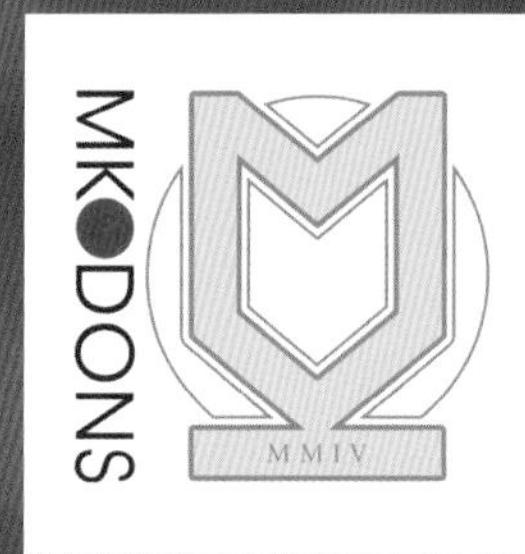

GROUND: *Stadium*mk **CAPACITY:** 30,500

MANAGER: Karl Robinson **NICKNAMES:** The Dons

DID YOU KNOW: The South stand of *Stadium*mk is known as the Cowshed by Dons' fans, as Milton Keynes is known for its Concrete Cows.

Nottingham Forest

GROUND: The City Ground **CAPACITY:** 30,576

MANAGER: Dougie Freedman **NICKNAME:** The Reds

DID YOU KNOW:
Forest's most successful period was under manager Brian Clough, between 1975 and 1993.

Preston North End

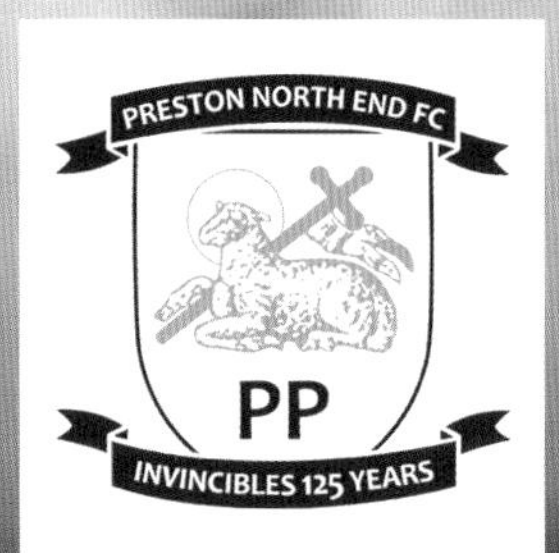

GROUND: Deepdale **CAPACITY:** 23,404

MANAGER: Simon Grayson

NICKNAMES: PNE, The Whites, The Invincibles

DID YOU KNOW: Preston were promoted to the Championship last season via the play-offs.

QPR

GROUND: Loftus Road **CAPACITY:** 18,489

MANAGER: Chris Ramsey **NICKNAME:** The Hoops

DID YOU KNOW:
QPR's main rivals are Chelsea, Fulham and Brentford, with whom they contest what are known as West London Derbies.

Reading

GROUND: Madejski Stadium **CAPACITY:** 24,161

MANAGER: Steve Clarke **NICKNAME:** The Royals

DID YOU KNOW:
Reading were previously known as the Biscuitmen, due to the town's association with Huntley and Palmers biscuit makers.

Rotherham United

GROUND: AESSEAL New York Stadium

CAPACITY: 12,021 **MANAGER:** Steve Evans

NICKNAME: The Millers

DID YOU KNOW:
The Chuckle Brothers are honorary presidents of Rotherham United!

Sheffield Wednesday

GROUND: Hillsborough Stadium **CAPACITY:** 39,732

MANAGER: Carlos Carvalhal **NICKNAME:** The Owls

DID YOU KNOW: Sheffield Wednesday were one of the founding members of the Premier League in 1992.

Wolves

GROUND: Molineux **CAPACITY:** 31,700

HEAD COACH: Kenny Jackett **NICKNAME:** Wolves

DID YOU KNOW:
Wolves have won the FA Cup four times - in 1893, 1908, 1949 and 1960!

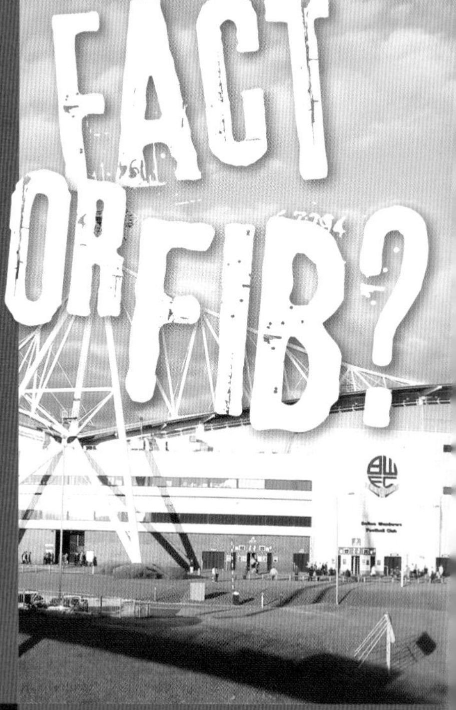

FACT OR FIB?

Lofty the Lion was originally going to be called Lionel.

1. FACT OR FIB?

Macron Stadium holds up to 25,000 fans.

2. FACT OR FIB?

The Trotters were founded in 1874 as Christ Church FC.

3. FACT OR FIB?

Derik has represented Mexico at youth level.

4. FACT OR FIB?

Before coming to Bolton, Neil Lennon was manger of Celtic.

5. FACT OR FIB?

In the last game of 2015, the Trotters face Blackburn Rovers.

6. FACT OR FIB?

Dean Moxey is a talented striker who made 20 League appearances last season.

7. FACT OR FIB?

Bolton Wanderers signed Frenchman, Dorian Dervite in the summer of 2014.

8. FACT OR FIB?

Whites' top goalscorer of all time was the great Nat Lofthouse. He scored 259 goals.

9. FACT OR FIB?

Bolton have won the FA Cup four times - in 1923, 1926, 1929 and 1958!

10. FACT OR FIB?

ANSWERS ON PAGE 62

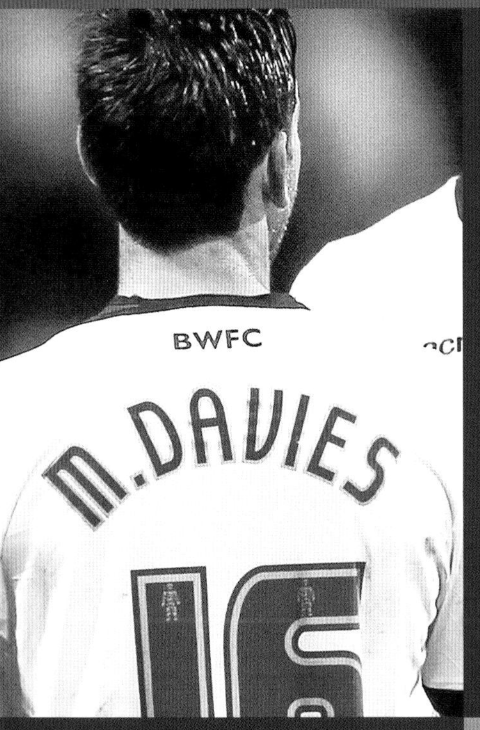

In 1884, Bolton Wanderers wore a white kit with red spots!

11. FACT OR FIB?

Trotters' top scorer last season was Craig Davies.

12. FACT OR FIB?

Mark Davies scored Bolton's final goal of the 2014/15 season against Brentford.

13. FACT OR FIB?

Liam Trotter celebrated his 23rd birthday this August.

14. FACT OR FIB?

The Whites most capped player is Ricardo Gardner with 72 caps for Jamaica while with the Club.

15. FACT OR FIB?

Neil Danns was born in Liverpool but is eligible to play internationally for Guyana.

16. FACT OR FIB?

Bolton Wanderers finished with 51 points last season.

17. FACT OR FIB?

Phil Neal was a Bolton manager of the 1970s.

18. FACT OR FIB?

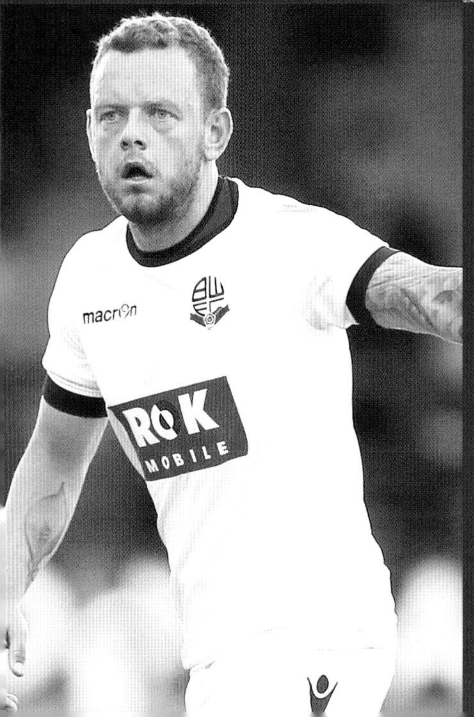

The Trotters' top all-time appearance maker is Eddie Hopkinson with 499 appearances

19. FACT OR FIB?

Jay Spearing was once captain of the Man United Under 18s team.

20. FACT OR FIB?

2

PRINCE

Can you name each mascot and work out the football club they belong to?

ANSWERS ON PAGE 62

FULL NAME?
Zach Paul John Clough

NICKNAME?
Cloughy

CHILDHOOD TEAM?
Manchester City

CHILDHOOD HERO?
Thierry Henry

YOUR BEST ATTRIBUTE AS A PLAYER?
Finishing

THE HIGHLIGHT OF YOUR CAREER SO FAR?
Debut goal against Wigan (the winner!)

THE FAVOURITE GOAL YOU HAVE SCORED?
Wigan, FA Cup

DESCRIBE YOURSELF IN THREE WORDS?
Quiet, calm, friendly

FAVOURITE AWAY GROUND?
Wembley

BEST FRIEND IN FOOTBALL?
Luke Woodland / Niall Maher

FULL NAME?
Liam Feeney

NICKNAME?
Feens

CHILDHOOD TEAM?
Arsenal

CHILDHOOD HERO?
Brazilian Ronaldo

YOUR BEST ATTRIBUTE AS A PLAYER?
Pace

THE HIGHLIGHT OF YOUR CAREER SO FAR?
Promotion with AFC Bournemouth

THE FAVOURITE GOAL YOU HAVE SCORED?
For Millwall against Southampton, FA Cup

DESCRIBE YOURSELF IN THREE WORDS?
Happy, grumpy, enigma

FAVOURITE AWAY GROUND?
Emirates

BEST FRIEND IN FOOTBALL?
Liam Trotter

DRAW A QUICK SELF PORTRAIT...

DRAW A QUICK SELF PORTRAIT...

FULL NAME?
Jay Spearing

NICKNAME?
Speo

CHILDHOOD TEAM?
Liverpool

CHILDHOOD HERO?
Steven Gerrard

YOUR BEST ATTRIBUTE AS A PLAYER?
Passing / tackling

THE HIGHLIGHT OF YOUR CAREER SO FAR?
FA Cup and Carling Cup finals

THE FAVOURITE GOAL YOU HAVE SCORED?
v Blackburn at home

DESCRIBE YOURSELF IN THREE WORDS?
Small, loud, lively

FAVOURITE AWAY GROUND?
Emirates

BEST FRIEND IN FOOTBALL?
Darby / Wheatz

FULL NAME?
Maximilian James Clayton

NICKNAME?
Max

CHILDHOOD TEAM?
Crewe Alexandra

CHILDHOOD HERO?
Michael Owen

YOUR BEST ATTRIBUTE AS A PLAYER?
Movement

THE HIGHLIGHT OF YOUR CAREER SO FAR?
Scoring at Wembley

THE FAVOURITE GOAL YOU HAVE SCORED?
Winner against Southend in Play-off semi-final

DESCRIBE YOURSELF IN THREE WORDS?
Hyperactive, smiley, happy

FAVOURITE AWAY GROUND?
Stamford Bridge

BEST FRIEND IN FOOTBALL?
Zach Clough

DRAW A QUICK SELF PORTRAIT...

Being a striker has its rewards... but it's more about guts than glory!

You have to put in the legwork to reap the benefits so here we give you some top tips for becoming a striker supreme.

1. **WORK HARD!**
   Play your heart out right up until the final whistle, you never know when that perfect cross will come your way.
2. **PASS THE BALL!**
   The object is for the team to score, not the individual, if someone else has a better opportunity, help them to take it.
3. **DON'T SACRIFICE ACCURACY FOR POWER!**
   No matter how hard you kick the ball, if a shot isn't on target, it's never going in.
4. **FOLLOW THROUGH!**
   Strike the ball with the laces of your boot and don't stop your leg motion once you've connected with the ball. If you swing your leg through it will give you more momentum.
5. **KEEP SHOTS LOW AND AIM FOR THE CORNERS!**
   These are the hardest areas for the goalie to protect.
6. **PRACTISE MAKES PERFECT!**
   Practise shooting at a small target like a pole or tree to improve your accuracy, you can gradually increase your distance from the object. Soon you'll be scoring from 25 yards!
7. **ATTACK AT EVERY CHANCE YOU GET!**
   Make the defensive team work, the more shots you have on target, the more likely you are to score.
8. **...BUT BE PATIENT!**
   Don't just shoot because the ball's at your feet, wait for chances, don't waste them.
9. **WORK ON BOTH FEET!**
   Practise shooting with both your strong and weak foot, this will help make you a good all-round player, the more skilled you are, the more opportunities will present themselves.
10. **HAVE CONFIDENCE IN YOURSELF!**
    If you get a chance, take it, if you think you can take your defender, go for it! Think fast and be decisive if you want to out-fox your opponent.

Nat Lofthouse

Bolton Wanderers' greatest ever player, Nat Lofthouse's prolific performances for club and country cemented his place as one of the all-time legends of English football.

Famously nicknamed 'The Lion of Vienna', the forward joined hometown club Bolton shortly after his 14th birthday in September 1939.

Scoring twice on his first appearance for the club against Bury in March 1941, it was a sign of things to come as Lofthouse would go on to finish his career Bolton's all-time leading scorer with 285 goals, and England's then record scorer with 30 goals from just 33 caps.

English Footballer of the Year in 1953 and a key member of England's 1954 World Cup squad, Lofthouse also captained the Trotters to their 1958 FA Cup Final success - scoring both goals in their 2-0 victory over Manchester United.

Hanging up his boots in 1960, Lofthouse remained at Wanderers in various roles from first team manager to club president, while a statue of him was unveiled outside Macron Stadium in August 2013.

Kevin Davies

Scorer of arguably the Whites' most famous ever goal, Kevin Davies was quickly proclaimed an adopted Boltonian after immediately endearing himself to supporters following his arrival at Wanderers in 2003.

Helping the club to the Carling Cup Final in his first season at the Reebok Stadium, he also helped Wanderers twice qualify for the UEFA Cup during his time at the club.

It was from one of Bolton's European exploits that Davies cemented his status as one of the Trotters' modern day legends, equalising against Bayern Munich at the Allianz Arena to secure a 2-2 draw, and write his name into club folklore in the process.

Eventually going on to captain the team, alongside earning a solitary England cap in 2010, his ten year association with the Whites came to an end in 2013.

Hanging up his boots in September 2015, Davies is set to bring down the curtain on his career once and for all with a testimonial at Macron Stadium.

John McGinlay

A cult hero during his time at Burnden Park, 'Super' John McGinlay was a key figure of the Wanderers side of the mid-nineties that won promotion three times, reached a major cup final and produced a number of cup shocks.

Signing for the Whites in September 1992, the forward's prolific form helped Bolton win promotion as Division Two runners-up, while he also scored at Anfield in the Trotters' famous FA Cup victory over Liverpool.

Registering 33 goals in 1993/94, his exploits in front of goal earned him an international debut for Scotland, while he continued that form into 1994/95 as the Trotters won promotion to the top-flight via the play-offs and reached the League Cup Final.

Hitting another 30 goals, including the last ever strike at Burnden Park, in 1996/97 as Wanderers returned to the Premiership as Division One champions, McGinlay left the club shortly after their move to the Reebok Stadium.

He can now be found commentating on the Whites' games for BBC Radio Manchester.

22

WELLINGTON SILVA

PUZZLE IT OUT

CAREER WATCH

Work out the missing teams in Dean Moxey's career.

2003-2009
Exeter City
2009-2011
2011-2014
2014 - Present
Bolton Wanderers

• A graduate of Bolton's youth academy
• Had his first team debut in January 2015
• Scored two goals on his first Championship start against Wolves
macron
ROK MOBILE

Who are yer?

Can you figure out who this Bolton star is?

DERBY DAY

Can you match each team to their rival?

1

2

3

4

HOMELANDS

Match the player to their home country

France	Francesco Pisano
Filip Twardzik	Sierra Leone
Spain	Liam Feeney
Dorian Dervite	Italy
England	Medo Kamara
Derik Osede	Czech Republic

ANSWERS ON PAGE 62

2016 CHALLENGE

We've set you a huge challenge for the new year!

Every month there are two new tasks to complete.

Have you got what it takes?!

JANUARY

- [ ] Do 25 keepy-uppies
- [ ] Come up with a new BWFC chant!

FEBRUARY

- [ ] Take a selfie at a Championship Stadium
- [ ] Learn a new trick - around the world!

MARCH

- [ ] Nutmeg someone!
- [ ] Get an autograph from a Bolton player

APRIL

- [ ] Do 50 keepy-uppies
- [ ] Take a selfie with a BWFC player

MAY

- [ ] Work on your fitness - run 1 mile!
- [ ] Lob the keeper

JUNE

- [ ] Learn a new trick - catch the ball on your neck
- [ ] Set up a sponsored event with your mates and do your bit for charity!

JULY

- [ ] Learn a new trick - keepy-uppies with a tennis ball
- [ ] Work on your fitness - run 3 miles!

AUGUST

- [ ] Take a selfie with a Bolton legend
- [ ] Do 75 keepy-uppies

SEPTEMBER

- [ ] Do 10 keepy-uppies on your head
- [ ] Try out for your school footie team

OCTOBER

- [ ] Shake Lofty the Lion's hand
- [ ] Take a selfie with Neil Lennon

NOVEMBER

- [ ] Work on your fitness - run 5 miles!
- [ ] Score from the penalty spot by hitting the underside of the crossbar

DECEMBER

- [ ] Do 100 keepy-uppies
- [ ] Start a chant at the match

ANSWERS

PAGE 26 STAND OUT FROM THE CROWD

Dorian Dervite, Dean Moxey, Neil Danns, Mark Davies and Zach Clough

STAND OUT FROM THE CROWD

PAGE 32 · GUESS THE CLUB

1. Queens Park Rangers, 2. Burnley, 3. Nottingham Forest, 4. Ipswich Town, 5. Wolverhampton Wanderers, 6. Sheffield Wednesday, 7. Middlesbrough, 8. Hull City, 9. Cardiff City, 10. Derby County

PAGE 35 · NAME THAT TEAM...

1. Robins - Bristol City, 2. Rovers - Blackburn Rovers, 3. Royals - Reading, 4. Boro - Middlesbrough, 5. Cottagers - Fulham, 6. Clarets - Burnley, 7. Bluebirds - Cardiff City, 8. Blues - Birmingham City, 9. Seagulls - Brighton and Hove Albion, 10. Terriers - Huddersfield Town, 11. Bees - Brentford, 12. Tigers - Hull City, 13. Whites - Leeds United, 14. Hoops - Queens Park Rangers, 15. The Dons - MK Dons, 16. Wolves - Wolverhampton Wanderers, 7. Millers - Rotherham United, 18. Owls - Sheffield Wednesday, 19. Forest - Nottingham Forest, 20. Trotters - Bolton Wanderers, 21. Lilywhites - Preston North End, 22. Tractor Boys - Ipswich Town, 23. Addicks - Charlton Athletic, 24. Rams - Derby County

PAGE 42 · MEGA PIXELS

1. Filip Twardzik, 2. Jay Spearing, 3. Stephen Dobbie, 4. Zach Clough, 5. Liam Feeney, 6. Dorian Dervite, 7. Derik Osede, 8. Dean Moxey, 9. Mark Davies

PAGE 45 · WHAT BALL?

Picture A - Ball 7, Picture B - Ball 4

PAGE 50 · FACT OR FIB?

1. Fib - his name originates from Bolton legend Nat Lofthouse, 2. Fib - the Macron Stadium's capacity is 30,208, 3. Fact, 4. Fib - He has represented Spain at youth level, 5. Fact, 6. Fact, 7. Fib - Dean Moxey is a defender, 8. Fact, 9. Fib - He scored 285 goals, 10. Fact, 11. Fact, 12. Fib - Adam Le Fondre was top scorer with eight goals, 13. Fact, 14. Fib - he celebrated his 27th, 15. Fact, 16. Fact, 17. Fact, 18. Fib - he was manager between 1985 and 1992, 19. Fib - he made 578 appearances, 20. Fib - he was the captain of the Liverpool U18s

PAGE 53 · MASCOT MANIA

1. Samson the Cat - Sunderland,
2. Captain Canary - Norwich City,
3. Fred the Red - Manchester United,
4. Barney Owl - Sheffield Wednesday,
5. Kop Cat - Leeds United,
6. Beau Brummie - Birmingham City,
7. Gunnersaurus - Arsenal,
8. Hammerhead - West Ham Utd

PAGE 59 · PUZZLE IT OUT

Career Watch

2009-2011: Derby County, 2011-2014: Crystal Palace

Who are yer?

Zach Clough

Derby Day

1. Derby County - Nottingham Forest,
2. Brighton & Hove Albion - Crystal Palace,
3. Ipswich Town - Norwich City,
4. Wolverhampton Wanderers - West Bromwich Albion

Homelands

Francesco Pisano - Italy, Filip Twardzik - Czech Republic, Liam Feeney - England, Dorian Dervite - France, Medo Kamara - Sierra Leone, Derik Osede - Spain